The Giant

Written by Sandra Clayton
Illustrated by Lucinda Hunnam

Once there was a giant who lived on a hill. At the bottom of the hill was a river, and beside the river was a village full of noisy, quarrelsome villagers.

Every afternoon, at five o'clock, the giant would come striding down the hill, across the river, and into the village.

Every afternoon, at five o'clock, the giant would stride up to a house, SHAKE! RATTLE! CRASH! and he would cry, "Bring me your wife, I'm hungry!" Or, "Bring me your son, I'm hungry!"

And every afternoon, just after five o'clock, with someone tucked under his giant arm, he would stride out of the village, across the river, and up the hill, while the villagers wailed and wept.

After five hundred and sixty-three and a half days of wailing and weeping, the villagers were sick of it.

"When is someone going to do something about it?" shouted the men.

"Someone should do something!" yelled the women.

"If someone doesn't do something," complained the children, "there'll be nobody left to look after us!"

The people milled and moiled angrily around the village square.

"We *could* go and get him . . ." the men bellowed, "but not today."

"It's all your fault!" the women screeched. And the girls pinched the boys, and the boys pushed the girls.

But the blind tailor, who used his fingers as eyes for sewing, and his ears as eyes for seeing, whispered to Jess, the beggar girl, "Only someone who is without hate can go. And that someone can only go when the moon hangs full in the sky and shadows chase dreams through the hearts of sleepers. And that someone must have a long stride and a head held high."

That same night, the moon hung full in the sky, and shadows chased dreams through the hearts of sleepers. Jess, the beggar girl, crept out of the village, and only the blind tailor knew that she had gone.

Across the river, up the hill, and through a forest of shadows she went, with a long stride and her head held high, while the grass whispered at her feet and shadows caught at her legs.

Because her stride was long, Jess was soon at the top of the hill. And because her head was held high, she saw the entrance to the giant's cave.

The cave looked dark and frightening. Jess knew that if she hesitated she would turn back, so she rushed straight into the cave's black mouth, feeling along the sides with her fingers, and stumbling on stones she couldn't see.

She groped her way along toward a tiny light that slowly got bigger and warmer, until at last she could see a giant kitchen where the giant sat hunched over his supper.

"Eat up, there's a good boy," called someone Jess couldn't see. "I'll just finish my knitting, then I'll fix us both a nice cup of tea."

The giant began shoveling food into his mouth. But who was he eating?

Jess felt her face grow hot and red with anger. Her hands picked up a big stone. Inside her head, a voice yelled, "I'll get that giant. I'll get that greedy, gorging, gobbling giant. BANG! SMASH! CRUNCH! He'll never eat another villager!"

She crept forward. She knew she could do it. She had only to climb up the rungs of the empty chair, scramble onto the table and knock the giant over the head. Then she stopped and shook her head. She walked a few steps and shook her head again. There was an echo she couldn't get rid of: *Only someone who is without hate can go.*

The stone fell from her hand with a clatter, but the clatter was only a small sound to a giant. He ate on.

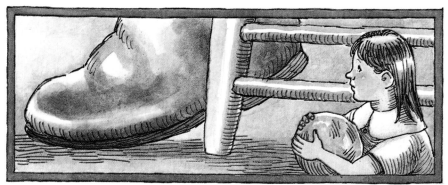

Then Jess grew afraid. Tears came to her eyes, and her body shook. She wanted to run back—back through the cave that was as black as the blind tailor's days—back through the forest of shadows, stumbling after dreams with her head down.

But she knew she must not. Trembling, Jess climbed up the rungs of the empty chair, scrambled onto the table, and strode with her head held high, straight to the giant's plate.

His spoon dropped with a CLANG! His mouth opened. His eyes bulged. He choked and coughed and spluttered.

"Mom, Mom," he bawled in a giant voice. "Come and see this!" Suddenly, he grabbed Jess and swung her up in the air. "Look what I've found!"

SHAKE! RATTLE! CRASH! came giant steps. Then two giant faces with mouths full of giant teeth looked down at her. Jess wriggled desperately in a giant fist. An even bigger fist reached down for her. Jess shut her eyes.

"What a dear!" cried Mom. "What a perfect little dear. Put her down, you great oaf. The poor thing's frightened."

"Yes, Mom," he said, meekly.

Over a cup of tea, which Jess drank out of the cap of a giant ketchup bottle, she explained why she had come.

"You must not eat any more villagers!" she cried, looking sternly at them. Then she remembered to add, "Please."

The two giants looked at each other, then burst out laughing. They laughed until tears spurted from Mom's eyes.

"Why, bless you," she said, "we're vegetarians! We don't eat any meat. Dearie me, no! The Stumblechum giants have always been vegetarians. A nice dish of sweet corn and potatoes, that's what we like to eat — or a nice juicy apple.

"No, no, that's just a bit of a joke. We got sick and tired of hearing those villagers of yours quarreling and fighting all the time — night and day. Yap, yap! Screech, screech! Thump, thump! There's no rest for a peaceable giant! So we just decided to take some of them away to start all over again on the other side of the hill."

"It was my idea, Mom," said her son, eagerly.

"So it was, dear." Mom winked at Jess. "He's smarter than he looks, is my boy Sonny. Come along, and we'll show you the other side."

She picked Jess up gently and popped her into the pocket of her apron. By standing on Mom's knitting, Jess could peer out of the pocket very well indeed.

Mom took a lantern from the table, and they set off toward a dark doorway at the back of the kitchen.

"Mind you," Mom continued, "it didn't stop those villagers from fighting, but we've about halved the noise, and the lot on the other side's better, with a bit of help from us. Of course, we could move to the other side ourselves, but I don't know. Stumblechum giants have always lived in this cave, and I reckon they always will. Maybe I could retire over on the other side when Sonny gets himself a wife." Mom winked, and dug Sonny in his giant ribs with her giant elbow.

"Come on, Mom, you'll never retire. You'll be bossing me *and* my wife around, five hundred years from now," said Sonny, and the two giants chuckled giant chuckles.

As they talked, they had been striding along a passage that twisted and turned, winding up and down through the hill.

Then suddenly they were out on the other side. Neat streets of houses were laid out beside a river, and each house had its own fruit and vegetable garden.

The sun was just beginning to rise. Roosters crowed, dogs barked, children whispered in their beds, and babies cried. A face peeked around a door, then the door burst open, and a tiny child hurtled over to them. "It's the Stumblechums!" he cried. "The Stumblechums are here!"

And all the time, the tiny child clung onto Sonny's foot, laughing and grinning. "Hi, Jess," the little boy called up, as Jess peered down. "I'm glad you came here."

Men, women, and children were crawling over the giants, who sat down with a thud on the damp grass. Everywhere, there were smiling faces and sparkling eyes.

"Glad you came, Jess," everyone cried. "We'll get a house started for you after breakfast."

After a while, the people went off to milk the goats, collect the eggs, gather the fruit, and eat breakfast. Only Jess remained, and she sat down on the grass and wept.

"Dearie me," cried Mom, in great distress. "What's wrong? Do you want us to take you back?"

"No! No! No!" said Jess, who had been pinched by the girls, pushed by the boys, and yelled at by the villagers all her life. "But I want you to promise me something." She wiped away her tears with the corner of Mom's knitting.

"Anything!" Mom cried. She put her head down on the grass beside Jess, and Jess crept over to Mom's giant ear and whispered into it.

That afternoon, at five o'clock, Sonny strode down the hill, across the river, and into the village for the last time, SHAKE! RATTLE! CRASH!

"Bring me your blind tailor!" he cried. "I'm hungry!"

Sonny tucked the blind tailor under his arm and off he went, out of the village, across the river, and up the hill, while the villagers wailed and wept.

And from that day on, the blind tailor, and Jess, the beggar girl, lived happily in the village on the other side of the hill.